If
Nathan Were Here

by Mary Bahr
Illustrated by Karen A. Jerome

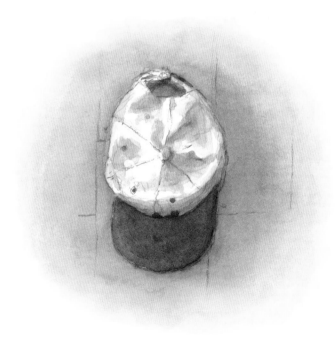

EERDMANS BOOKS FOR YOUNG READERS
Grand Rapids, Michigan / Cambridge, U.K.

For Zach and his friend, Nathan—M.B.

To my painting teacher, Joanne F. Regan—K.J.

Text copyright 2000 by Mary Bahr

Illustrations copyright 2000 Karen A. Jerome

Published 2000 by Eerdmans Books for Young Readers

An imprint of Wm. B. Eerdmans Publishing Company

255 Jefferson S.E., Grand Rapids, Michigan 49503

P.O. Box 163, Cambridge, CB39PU U.K.

Printed in Hong Kong

05 04 03 02   7 6 5 4 3

Library of Congress Cataloging-in-Publication Data

Bahr, Mary.

If Nathan were here / written by Mary Bahr : illustrated by Karen Jerome.

p.   cm.

Summary: A young boy grieves the loss of his best friend and thinks about how things would be if he were still alive.

ISBN 0-8028-5187-8 (cl. : alk. paper)

ISBN 0-8028-5235-1 (pbk : alk. paper)

1. Grief Fiction. 2. Death Fiction. I. Jerome, Karen A., ill. II. Title.

PZ7.F91868If 2000

E – dc21 99-39909

CIP

Book designed by Amy Drinker, Aster Designs

The illustrations were done in watercolor.

The text type was set in 14–point Janson.

If Nathan were here, we would meet in our tree fort to choose which team hats to wear from our Baseball Hat Wall of Fame.

And if we met early and were quiet, we would watch his sister, Mary Kate, warming up her pitching arm before school.

And if she didn't hear us climb down, we would hide and wait and whisper how we're telling Roger Winney she's a better ballplayer than he is.

And if Mary Kate whacked us with her backpack like she does
every day of our lives, we would take the shortcut through the woods.

And if it rained the night before, we would try to splash each other in the puddles.

On our way, we'd nibble Mr. Potter's strawberries and practice our show-and-tell speeches where nobody could see us.

And if our speeches were good enough to make the squirrels stand still, they'd probably be good enough to make the class stand and cheer.

And if anybody cheered for Nathan, he would add a demonstration to his speech.

And if Nathan demonstrated pitching, especially the Mary Kate kind, the whole class would laugh because Nathan does that to people.

And if the whole class laughed, so would Miss Brickley because she's that kind of teacher.

But Nathan isn't here. And nobody's laughing.

Miss Brickley is explaining how we can fill a Memory Box with "all the best things we remember about Nathan." She starts us off. "I like the way Nathan made us laugh. So I'm putting in a photograph of one time he did."

"I like the way he slid into home plate," Peter says. "Can I draw a picture of that?"

"Great idea," Miss Brickley says.

Nina raises her hand. "I always liked the banana sandwiches he traded at lunch. I could make a recipe card."

"How about questions?" Rico asks. "Can we put questions in the Memory Box? Then write the answers Nathan might give us?"

My teacher wipes her eyes before she answers. "Certainly. What kinds of questions should we ask?"

Lots of hands go up and the questions start rolling.

I have only one question for Nathan. But I don't raise my hand. Miss Brickley looks at me, but she doesn't ask. She knows I'll talk to Nathan in my own time. In our tree fort.

After school, I pull the rim of my baseball hat low and follow

Mary Kate home, but I hide behind the bushes when she turns around.

I cut through our woods because I feel like hitting puddles
with a stick.

I sit beside Mr. Potter's garden and he joins me. Neither of us eats as many strawberries as Nathan usually did.

I toss my backpack on the kitchen table and tell Dad I'm going to the tree fort. I let him squeeze me a little.

I climb the rope ladder and pull
it up behind me. Then I touch each
hat on our Wall of Fame.

I grab Nathan's favorite bat and lie
beside it on our dreaming rug. Nathan
was a dynamite hitter. Like Mary Kate.

I close my eyes and think about
the Memory Box questions at school
today. "Do you still pack trading cards
in your lunch?" "Do you still have
homework or is it always recess up
there?" "Were you scared?"

Finally, I ask my question. "What
am I supposed to do without my
best friend?"

Then I wait and listen to the silence.

After a while, I hear a noise below. I look through my peephole.
It's only Mary Kate. She's easy to ignore so I go back to my dreaming
rug. I remember how Nathan always tapped the rim of his hat and said
"'til next season" when things were great. And I wish he were here to
say it now.

Then I hear Dad call me for dinner.

After dinner, Nathan's mom lets me take his dog for a walk.

Yogi sniffs every place Nathan used to stop along the way.

The next morning is crazy with sunshine. I wonder if Nathan's making it laugh. I rush to the fort and pull up the ladder.

I've decided to take a hat for Nathan's Memory Box.

But which one?

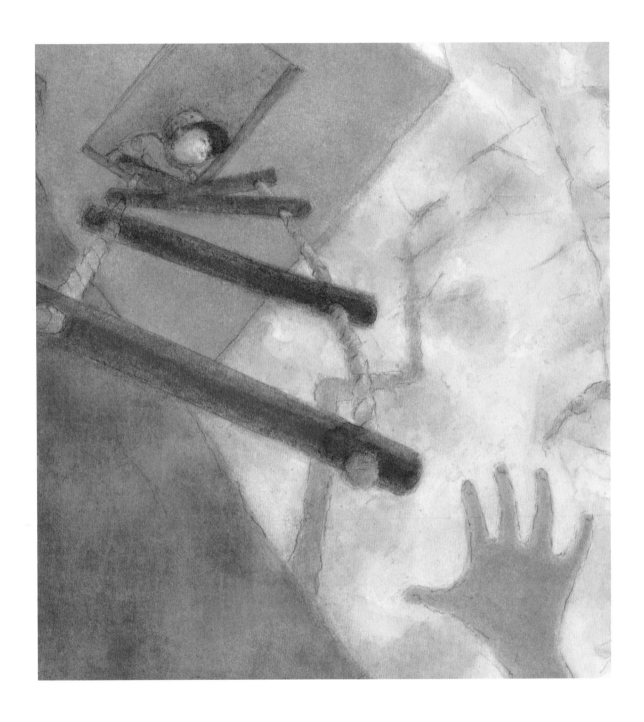

There's noise below. I peek through the peephole. It's Mary Kate.
Nathan never wanted his sister up here before. I'm thinking—maybe
he'd like her up here now.